BEST SERVED SHARP

A FANTASY STORY

JONATHAN EVAN HUDSON

Copyright © 2026 by Jonathan Evan Hudson

All rights reserved.

No part of this book may be reproduced in any form or by any electronic or mechanical means, including information storage and retrieval systems, without written permission from the author, except for the use of brief quotations in a book review.

❀ Formatted with Vellum

BEST SERVED SHARP

CHAPTER I
WARREN LOCK

Vengeance. Best served sharp—and from behind.

And the endless roar of that short waterfall—a waterfall so short a gangly young tween could barely fit underneath it—and once, years ago, the perfect cover for him, for Warren Lock, too.

The noise mingled with the girlie giggles of young ripe girls in their prime. Awfully familiar giggles. From girls famous these last few years for their stunning beauty in all of Trifacto.

Not just Woodcrest Valley.

Or even Greensap Village, their home village. His own once too.

All. of. Trifacto.

A playful splash here and there. More giggles and playful cries. They all came from a little pool of clear azure-blue water up ahead. A pool in a little lumpy crater of dark granite boulders. Boulders covered with thick soft pale-blue moss.

But thick azure-blue mist still hazed most the pool from here. From a dozen paces away.

A mist with a sharp hint of familiar mysterious mint.

Mintwood was a pathetically sweet forest full of craggy tall but thin oaks, full of thin crooked pine trees. That strong earthy pine scent should hide Warren and his all-too-human and all-too-familiar scent from his overly lovely targets.

More than enough sunlight reached the ground in speckled splatters. Lit the way over the thick carpet of dead orange needles. Needles that so many Greensap villagers loved to make their awful local tea from.

Just like how the noisy songbirds all around him—the same as back then too.

All so stupidly wonderful Warren almost cackled out loud.

But no.

Not yet.

But soon. Soon it would be time to strike.

The noisy songbirds fell silent. And so quickly too.

Except for a few stupid sparrows.

So Warren slipped through the straggly brush of thin green thorn vines at the base of the towering ferns. Scarlet ferns well over his own height. Passed the annoyingly cute pink roses with their awfully strawberry sweet and creamy stink. Passed those puffy bushes of rainbow-colored serrated leaves.

Now the last of the sparrows fell silent.

Except for the ripping leaf sounds. From sparrows fainting from fear.

As they should.

Added a nice bitter fowl touch.

His wiry thin body tingled all over. Chilled to the icy bone. All from the massive amount of magic stored within his special red robe of sleek snake scales—more like brilliant scarlet dragon scales shred from his first wife, Alexis Scalehart, and alchemied into this wonderful artifact as a dowry.

Magic poured into him. Stirred within him.

As if Warren had too much blood pulsating inside him.

As if it was trying to burst out. Aching old cuts across his chest.

The only cuts he ever suffered. All that suffering. All that searing agony.

All due to that wretched wannabe swordsman Ace de Saber. That blue-haired freak from that disgraced de Saber bloodline no less!

Yes.

That disgraced petty prince of a worthless little nothing of a kingdom. A kingdom that rejected and casted out him and all his ilk. Clinging to their outdated religion despite Cardinal Blessed' generous offerings.

The Church of the Lawful Helm should have just forcefully converted them all and be done with it.

That's why Ace wasn't even a proper noble. No. More common than the mud on Warren's boots. Ace was a mutt of human and elf blood—with some dwarf thrown in for bad measure.

Now time to capture all of those overly lovely girls—all pure elves too.

All three of his wives yearned, wished for their personal elf girl servants to feast on—after all, pure-blooded elf girls had healing so great it was outright regenerative. So, of course, elf girls made the perfect everlasting snack for dragon kind.

So a step through the wall of scarlet ferns he ... a girl's back? To him? Already!

Good.

Ferns shielded his back. Azure-blue mist shielded both Warren and his target from the pool and all the giggling girls in it. Not just from sight. But how muffled those giggles were. So distant. All thanks to the mist.

Even her scream would never be noticed.

No need for his second wife Raven Shadowclaw to jump to his aid. Yet. Raven could slip into, hid inside, and travel between shadows nearby shadows.

But his first target was only an arm's reach away.

And no mistaking that peaches and cream stink of hers. Its jabbing hint of fern leaf stink too. Her natural elf girl stink. All wood elves had a fruity stink to them. Extra strong from this one too. Since it was extra hot today. Here. Midsummer.

A stink that matched her annoyingly perfect peaches and cream complexion far too much.

No doubt left—thee one and only Leaflet Peaches.

Right in front of him.

An elf girl of the wood race and many idiot guys' lust dream come true. Looking oh-so-human except for those thin dainty dagger-like ears a few inches long. Each jutting straight out the sides of her dainty stupid head.

Wood elves like her looked oh-so-human but elves, and especially Leaflet, her beauty, it was oh-so-stunningly-*in*human. An hourglass to so many fools' daydreams. Wasting their hopes and efforts.

Soon to be their doom too.

The azure-blue mist billowed closer. Hiding the two of them even more from the giggling girls already in the pool. Giggling now even more muted by the mist—just as expected.

So no one saw him. Sensed him.

Yet.

Thanks to his third wife, Storm Talonwind, and her powers to control water in all its many forms. From fog to ice, but especially regular water.

But Storm refused to do what Warren must do, prove he could do now.

Leaflet's slim arms were raised high. Messing with that ass-long golden hair.

But what wasn't covered—those awfully nice hints of her huge tits from the sides. Tits that weren't so big last time he last saw her a few years ago, on her way to that all-girls academy, Oakengal Academy.

And now, returning from that academy, those stunningly bare legs—so much more desirable than a few years ago.

This close up. This stupidly unaware of him.

No wonder all three of his wives begged Warren to capture all these all-too-famous elf girls for them. So of course Warren would do so. Anything less would insult the one who granted him these three wonderful wives.

That strongest of all-powerful dragons: King Alder Kill.

Those elf girls were peasants after all. Dragons and their kind could hunt peasants as much as they liked. Only true nobles were granted the chance to gain the title of dragonsworn. Granted equal standing to dragon kind.

So all that training under a supposed legendary weapons master? Wasted here on Leaflet.

But not for much longer ...

CHAPTER 2
LEAFLET PEACHES

Finally back in Greensap!

Leaflet Peaches was even at her favorite swimming pond no less—Cool Crater Pool.

Still hidden by a circular wall of towering high scarlet ferns Cool Crater Pool was a natural pool of cozy hot and amazingly beautiful aqua-blue water. More like a small natural crater of it. Lumpy but smooth boulders of dark granite forever lounging in and around the pool. The parts above water often covered in nice and soggy soft moss as blue as the sky was today.

Moss perfect for laying down on. Or just sitting cozy on.

Like resting on soggy silk.

Better than anything at that atrocious all-girls academy, Oakengal Academy.

Warm and wonderfully gooey mud squished and embraced her bare toes and yet Leaflet Peaches couldn't help but stand there, by the edge of the pool and just fiddle with her annoyingly loooong hair, as in ass-freaking-long hair, since, of course, her healing was so good it was outright regenerative healing—like most elf girls and sigh, it also made hair cuts an exercise in utter futility.

It was as futile as washing away her awfully elven peaches and cream scent during this incredibly humid summer afternoon.

Too bad her elven girlfriends Dazzle Sparkles and Rosaline Applehart had both already given up on that futility and had gone in ahead of Leaflet.

Even Sky Frostfire—and she was the most mature of them all.

The bright blue fog common in Mintwood had settled down extra thick and creamy today. So thick and creamy it was like breathing one of those mint gooey candies Miss Ladle loved to make everyone years ago.

(Well, before Leaflet and the other elf girls got sent to Oakengal.)

Leaflet, no matter how hard she tried, couldn't see passed a few paces today. Dark-blue shadows of mossy boulders before her now. Boulders spread steps apart and easily navigated, but ... easily lost in too, with this kind of fog.

Ace de Saber ... her closest childhood guy friend in Greensap ... he was even a woods guide back then, years ago, before she left for Oakengal. Maybe he still was. So if she got lost maybe he'd find her—even if she was utterly stupidly naked and that ... super awkward.

Heart wrenchingly throbbing awkward.

But still, of course, the bright aqua-blue water right before her beckoned for another elf to go swimming ...

Only weeks ago Leaflet and all her elven girlfriends—not just Dazzle and Rosaline but that naive but super-sweet sweetheart Starlet Bubbles, that cocky cute martial arts geek Cellow Xaio, and even that stuffy and overly mature Sky Frostfire—they all posed nearly naked for more drawies—pricey but popular black and white illustrations that moved on their own through magic woven into the inks and parchment.

Even reacting to the viewer too.

Unlike the amazingly flat surface of this pool. No reflection. No ripples.

Just like a perfectly flat and smooth floor of aqua blue. Kinda like some of the many traps tucked hidden away in that dungeon of dastardly monsters Leaflet regularly had to adventure into for training thanks to the demands of Oakengal Academy.

A nice bath after all that looong traveling. Traveling on foot.

Not even woodrifting—entering, and traveling within, and through plant matter. Something all wood elves could do. Some better than others but it was as easy as breathing or walking now.

Or should be ... but ... sigh. Starlet kinda sortof struggled with it. Both Sky and Leaflet could do it but not, well ... (weird how those fake elves, those alves, could do it better than some real elves. Alves resembled elves on the outside but on the inside ... all sinister serpent.)

((More like dastardly dragons.))

So well ... walking back they went!

All that sky-blue moss here. It could make for some nice woodrifting practice.

Least posing for drawies paid really well. Drawies had to be made live. No pose once and done. Nope. The magic was cast as the girls posed and moved as instructed.

So lots of inns to stop by and pay for food and stuff.

Leaflet and her friends were all drawie models so they all were now kinda sortof famous, especially among guys everywhere, for reasons ... awkward and embarrassing but least she was never short of admirers, and plenty of gifts and freebies and ... still not a date. Not yet.

(Thanks to going to a stupid all girls school for the last several years. Mostly.)

Wow. Heart thumping loud and clear.

Today the pool was amazingly quiet too. No birds. No critters chitter at all.

Only the laughter of her girlfriends broke the silence— and their splash sparring. Sparring Leaflet really, *really* wanted to join in, but ... sigh. Cellow would so go serious martial arts on them all. Sky trying to calm everyone down. Freezing things here and there by accident and calling it intentional.

Until Starlet blasted everything with her violet energy blast by pure accident.

So Leaflet better deal with her disaster of way-too-freaking-long hair now and ... maybe give up—no.

Like Master Hammer, that sassy stout dwarf and weapons master extraordinaire often said: Never give up!

Above her the sun bathed in in its bright light.

More like cooked her extra stinky but so what? Ace, and other boys, especially Ace's best buddy, that scrappy dwarf boy Iron Rake, claimed to like her stink.

Like it too much, actually, but ... soon.

Soon Leaflet and all her elven girlfriends would begin their mandatory three years of service as Alitroopers. Soldiers serving under their beloved gods, the Alicorned Ones. Even if Ace and Iron loved to call Alicorned Ones unicorns. Basically white talking horses with a horn from their forehead and a pair of eagle wings from their back, but no.

Their horn was spiraled special. Their wings special like eagles but better and and and ...

Technically Ace could choose to join them since he was clearly part elf but ... all their letters, some on drawies, and no response. As if he didn't get them—or now hated Leaflet and her girlfriends like some weird guys did.

As Alitroopers Leaflet and her girlfriends would be tasked to defend elves, humans, and dwarves from dragons and their minions. Protect the lands called Sanctuaries. Lands protected against the full might of dragons thanks to the Alicorned Ones and so ...

All Alitroopers were gifted an amazingly sweet saber of spiraled alicorn. From a horn freshly shed by an Alicorned One.

Ace claimed to always have wanted one and ... well ... he

dreamed of being some kind of hero back many years ago. Still trained in secret (least what he thought was secret.) Least back before Leaflet and all her elven girlfriends got sent away.

But fighting dragons for the sake of it?

He once dreamed of it. Played the dragon-born-slaying hero, along with his best buddy Iron, while Leaflet and her girlfriends Dazzle and Rosaline—sometimes even Sky—played the damsels in distress.

Sometimes Dazzle went alf girl femme fatale too.

Rosaline too, going succubus femme fatale all the overly sassy sexy way—even body painted herself as scarlet-skinned as a real succubus. Throwing on black horns and black bat wings from the nap of her back spanning the length of her arms.

Leaflet sighed. Those were some fun days but now he … Ace … no.

Ace was an All Grandest. One of the few creeds of humans dragons spared in their lands. Used as translators, healers, and more. So dragons and their minion actually came to Ace, once in a while, for his woods guide services and he actually had accepted their requests!

Despite Leaflet, her elven girlfriends, sigh.

Dragons and elves were enemies to the end so …

Leaflet sighed. Don't overthink everything. Just walk right in and enjoy the peaceful moments.

Before tomorrow.

Before they got the details of their first mission. Since no blabbering about details she, or her girlfriends, didn't know yet so …

Gulp.

CHAPTER 3
WARREN LOCK

Despite Warren being less than a step behind that wretched elf girl Leaflet Peaches...

Despite the silence of Mintwood around them ...

Despite the obviousness of the coming attack ...

Leaflet merely sighed. Her voice. Still bubbly sweet but now, a few years later, even lyrical.

"Nothing beats," Leaflet said, "a sun bath followed by a little swim."

A glance up and huh? The sun. It beamed down on both Leaflet and Warren. Bright and clear—despite the blue mist thickening around them?

Ha!

A blessing from the Lawful Helm himself. The creator of all things. The ruler of all.

He must be blessing Warren for what he was about to do.

His thin spiraled dagger—one of several as the dowry from his second wife. Its light feel. Its perfect balance. Now so full of Warren's magic its once-silver-steel blade glowed a wonderful brilliant crimson.

Now drawn. Ready. Other hand empty.

Until he grabbed Leaflet's shoulder.

Clamping down on her.

Hard.

"Who?!" Leaflet said. "Wha—I know this touch!"

Her gasp. "Warren?! How dare you—"

"Dare you get me banished!" Warren said. "Time to make up for it. You. Your girlfriends. And that **atrocious** Ace de Saber!"

"Leave them alone!" Leaflet said.

She swirled around. Elbow out. Swerving around. Trying to ram her elbow into his gut.

And her power. As a wood elf. More than enough to cripple him.

If he wasn't ready.

But he was ready.

More than ready.

His magical touch. Its chill. He soaked it into her shoulder. Slowed her whole body down instantly.

Drastically.

No other defense needed. She was so, so slow. She might as well try to turn, to fight through a vat of thick gooey honey.

Her fruity stink struck him harder.

"Pathetic," Warren said. "And you were trained by the best? Ha!"

Leaflet strained underneath his hand. Her elbow even closer to his gut now. Barely a hand-length away now.

But nowhere close enough.

Yet.

"Master Hammer *is* the best!" Leaflet said. "And I'll prove —ack!"

Warren daggered Leaflet right up between her shoulder blades.

Right through her pathetic weak heart.

But with her kind's amazing healing, outright regenerative, even a potentially fatal strike needed time to become fatal.

Or in this case, weaken her enough for the next step.

Those famously huge lime-green eyes turned. Glared wide at him. That overly famous heart of a cute baby face.

So, so famous.

And soon, all *all* **his**. His to gift to his wonderful three wives —after he used these elves for his own purposes—and revenge.

And thanks to the mist closing in—none of her allies else would know.

Until it was too late—for them.

No wonder so many artists threw chest loads of coin at this stupidly beautiful elf girl to draw her in slutty poses. Secret spells and potions mixed in with the inks and parchment made those drawings move about all slinky slutty for foolish weak boys. React in simple ways to the boys too.

Boys who then spent even more coin to get more and more of those drawies, as they called those moving drawings.

Just like they did for all the other top drawie models.

Like Dazzle. Especially Dazzle with her ass-long and exotically pink hair.

Leaflet was voted by all those desperate pathetic boys as Miss Most Gorgeous of Our Generation. Tied with that giggling blonde idiot Starlet Bubbles, of course, since no accounting for taste among losers.

Dazzle and Sky both only lost due to their "exotic" hair being too exotic for some boys. Just like how Cellow lost for her almond-shaped eyes and flatter than usual face. Too exotic for even more boys.

That ravishing redheaded Rosaline lost to her overly cocky attitude. Too cocky for some of those pathetic boys.

So many models here. So many to share Leaflet's fate.

Their drawies would soon restore his family's fortune as well.

Especially when he converted all of them to the Church of the Lawful Helm, and received all the riches that came with such a victory.

A wind rustled the ferns and yet those whispers, like beautiful little blessings.

Good. The Lawful Helm confirmed once again how righteous Warren was.

So focus. Careful.

Leaflet was still as powerful, as skilled in the sword as she was beautiful. Trained by that legend of legends, that weapons master, known as Hammer. Ace's wretched uncle no less.

That Leaflet could resist Warren this well, even after this heart strike, spoke volumes toward her amazing stamina.

Still. Warren smirked down at the cringing Leaflet. At her pathetic resistance.

"Don't worry ... too much," Warren said. "Dazzle and Rosaline—and *all* the others—will join you soon enough. And—"

"Warren you ..." Leaflet said. "I ... killing me? Like this?"

"You trampled my heart!" Warren said. "And more. You ... you won't die. Not here."

"One dance ..." Leaflet said. "Out of pity and this—ack!!!"

Warren twisted the dagger.

Wrenched it hard.

And that loud wet crack from within her. Her gasp and whimper.

Good. Only so much stamina should be left in her now.

"Pity?!" Warren said. "I never wanted pity! You'll soon know what I want. You all will."

"Warren ... I ..." Leaflet said.

"You'll *wish* I killed you," Warren said. "But no mercy to lowly **peasant** *SCUM!!!*"

Her next gasp.

Certainly her last.

CHAPTER 4
ACE DE SABER

The moment a whiff of that familiar elven musk of peaches and cream with that unique hint of sweet nippy fern leaf hit him Ace de Saber just *knew* serious trouble otherwise known as Leaflet Peaches was about to rear her erotically gorgeous head once again.

And normally he wouldn't have it any other way.

Normally.

Since, normally, guys lusted for Leaflet like dragons lusted for gold. Like Dark Lords lusted for world conquest.

No. More.

Way too much more.

Even Ace. *Especially* Ace.

A dream for far way too many guys everywhere.

And exactly why, a few several years ago, the Five Elders of Greensap Village sent all those stunningly lovely elf girls to an isolated all-girl's school known as Oakengal Academy.

And why, at this very moment, Ace foolishly started to fondle the solid bone grip of both his slim steel sabers. Sabers both sheathed tight in dark-blue leather and strapped snuggly to his waist.

And yet he fondled those grips the very same way he wanted to fondle Leaflet's thightastic thighs and ... well ... you know, with Cool Crater Pool up ahead ... Ace stopped here often, especially after another woods guide job took him far away from Greensap.

Good way to refresh himself after a long trip back.

But this time, today, his heart boomed as loud as the thunder in the distance. Just out of pure foolish hope that maybe, more than friends, now, maybe, with Leafet, with Dazzle and Rosaline, maybe too, and Sky—since why not?

Full elf girl harem funsies.

But the towering high wall of scarlet ferns up ahead blocked the way as much as reality did. Ferns a few to several feet above his own height and he was no short guy.

And the wall of scarlet ferns was much further than they appeared. Still a decent ways away. Top of the next hill. A hill at least a few dozen feet above the dip before him.

Thanks to the rolling hills here. It was easily to miss the long deep dip in the path.

Easier easier to miss the hill entirely. The azure-blue fog rarely cleared up enough to see it at all. Let alone from on top of this hill.

And Ace wasn't just a woods guide.

He also had a decade of training in the sword thanks to Uncle Hammer, and Uncle Hammer and Aunt Ladle were more like his parents than uncle and aunt ever since his actual parents vanished well over a decade ago but ...

Both Uncle Hammer and Aunt Ladle were among the five Elders of Greensap.

Both of them were stout stubborn dwarves. Both seemed as old as Greensap as well.

(No telling if they really were but ... sigh.)

Sure, around this little winding dirt path only locals knew about—and Ace helped keep it that way by never showing his clients anything near this place—here there were lovely pink roses blooming all along the sides. Fragrant sweet and creamy roses blooming from thin thorny vines entangled with the many waist-high green ferns.

But plucking a few of these lovely pink roses and ... no.

Fresh roses never swayed any dwarf. His mom, yeah, more often than not but she wasn't a dwarf. Not entirely.

But never Aunt Ladle. No matter how much she claimed to love these roses ...

Sure Leaflet, Sky, and Rosaline loved these roses—sometimes Dazzle but her rosy pink hair didn't actually show pink roses well—and no sign of any being plucked recently either, and they loved weaving these roses in their long hair so ... strange to scent Leaflet here too.

Not without more signs of her passing by.

It wasn't like there were many dirt paths here but wood elves like Leaflet and her girlfriends could woodrift—enter as if absorbed by the plants and then travel through them, or even stay within them—so they could easily go through these troublesome thorny rose vines. Through the ferns too. Green and scarlet.

No need for them to stick to regular pathways.

Least if they traveled only with other wood elves. Probably they did too.

Orange needles covered, and softened the already soft dark soil like most places here in Mintwood. The only footprints in the soil came from a set of thick leather-soled boots. Leaflet and the others usually went with soft leather boots. Their feet were slimmer too. Far slimmer than these footprints.

The azure-blue mist was getting thicker today too.

Within moments it now so thick it was now like the minty cream sauce Aunt Ladle loved to whip up with nearly every dish. Why the mist throughout the forest smelled so minty, and the reason this forest was named Mintwood, both Uncle Hammer and Aunt Ladle hint-hinted that they both knew but refused to tell him.

Not ready yet—whatever that meant.

But Ace was definitely ready to see Leaflet again. See Dazzle, Sky, and Rosaline again too.

Even if Leaflet didn't reply to any of his letters. Dazzle, Sky, and Rosaline hadn't either but ...

Maybe they got too busy to reply. Oakengal had a notorious reputation for being difficult. Adventuring in a custom dungeon full of monsters included as part of their education —all to train physically and learn about wildlife and magic and whatnot.

Crazy. Reading about it first would make more sense but

what did he know?

He even had a whole collection of their sexy awesome drawies—least all the ones carried by the merchants who had passed by Greensap, and plenty did.

Greensap was on several trading routes through Mintwood, after all.

His best buddy, and sturdy dwarf among dwarves, Iron Rake collected all those drawies too, and then some. Including the entire card game designed around those drawies. A card game that was constantly evolving with new cards and wow, did Ace waste too much time on that game.

Iron too.

All the boys in Greensap did. Least those with no wife, or girlfriend, to stop them.

(Interesting question—would Leaflet stop Ace if they well ... you know ... Dazzle definitely wouldn't. She was too much a bubbly flirt to do that. But no telling with the sexy sensual and sassy Rosaline. But Sky—yeah, definitely.)

Wait.

Now that Ace was headed down into the last dip before the last rise and the wall of scarlet ferns ... oh no.

Within the fern and tangled rose vines. Not a single sparrow was tweeting. None at all. And sparrows loved to tweet among the roses like crazy. Plenty of bugs for them to eat and celebrate their good fortune.

A closer look at those roses, at the ferns tangled by them, at the dark soil underneath, and ...

A dead sparrow?

No.

Several sparrows. More than several.

Ace crouched down. Got a closer look. They seemed to be breathing. Twitching some. So they were still alive.

But unconscious?

Something was off. There were stray monsters here in Mintwood. No telling where those monsters came from.

But avoiding them rather than hunting them often proved best.

Especially when those monsters tended to keep the bandit population down better than any bandit hunter. From the mysterious and yet stunningly gorgeous bandit hunter known as the Ravishing Ravager to Ace himself as the mysterious but heroic bandit hunter, Phantom Jester.

He became the Phantom Jester thanks to wiping out a particularly nasty set of bandits years ago and saving a certain pair of feisty feline genie girls from more slavitude as some secret savage weapon.

A weapon Ace now wielded himself, from within himself, but only with the consent of those very same feline genie girls, Amber and Scarlet Blaze, who ... let's say ... often had interesting and unusual ... tastes, yes, tastes but they were so adorable who cared?

But no monster would make sparrows pass out like that. Not without killing them. So what, or more like who ...

Time to wait the Blaze sisters up and—someone screamed.

"Scum!"

That voice. A whiny rotten voice of an all-too-familiar

someone. Someone Ace never wanted to ever see, let alone fight ever again.

Warren Lock.

Even now. After Ace gained the powers from wielding Amber and Scarlet.

But Ace didn't hesitate.

He dashed right toward the scream. And that awful voice.

CHAPTER 5
ACE DE SABER

As fast as Ace dashed he couldn't dash fast enough.

The rolling hills. Only some of the dirt path left winding downward—the temptation to leap over ferns and roses to shortcut his way down ... almost too tempting but no—that would end up slowing him down even more.

Soon one last rise. Soon.

But not fast enough. Nowhere near fast enough.

His soft-leather boots pounded the soft soil. His gaze sought for an undiscovered shortcut to the wall of scarlet ferns. But no. None. He sprinted down the little dirt path. Down and down and down. Hoping beyond hope that Leaflet, that whoever that wretched Warren was troubling could hold out a little longer.

Long enough for him to reach them.

Reaching the last dip in the pathway.

Then dashing up and up and up. No matter how much it zigged and zagged. Twisted and turned. Thorns ripped at his slacks. Pricks his legs whenever he sprinted too close.

So up and up and up along the rolling hill of dirt and boulders. Boulders Ace didn't have time to use. To use in any way. Let alone a helpful way. His strength training of moving hefty granite boulders around … not useful here yet.

Only a wood elf would try to plunging through those thorny vines—and not be tangled to a complete awful stop. So Ace trying to rip through the entangled the waist-high ferns around the path. No. That would only slow him down. Slow him down a lot.

Stop him completely, maybe. he didn't have enough elf blood to woodrift through anything.

No.

Unless … he summoned Amber right this instant. Wielded her flames carefully.

Burned a straight path to the wall of scarlet ferns.

Revealing his presence to that wicked warlock.

Revealing Ace now had magical abilities as well.

So burning a path all the way to Warren … no. Only a few more moments and he'd reach the scarlet ferns. Plunge through them quick and fiercely. The roses here were fragrant enough to hide any other scents.

Even Ace's own potent mint and vanilla one.

So burning anything here. Definitely far too smelly. Smokey too. Whether rose, fern, or pine needle.

It would only warn that wicked warlock someone else was here.

That that someone could wield magic of their own.

Someone intent on crushing that creep once again. Free any more victims he enslaved to help him along the way—

"WATCH OUT!!!" Amber screamed in his ear?! "THE SHADOWS!!!"

CHAPTER 6
DAZZLE SPARKLES

Dazzle Sparkles strolled along the rocky shoreline of Cool Crater Pool.

The wonderful fluffy soft moss cuddled against her bare feet with each and every step. Moss as pale blue as the sky normally was except the mist here was so thick ... a beautiful azure blue that here, always, it hid the sky so too completely.

The bright blue water of the hot spring to her right—so tempting to jump back in.

Nope!

Not yet.

Wowie was it as flat and smooth as mirror unscratched by nail or claw, and almost as reflective—despite the moss-covered boulders jutting out of it here and there, cluttering the water here more than the other side over a dozen paces away.

Least the moss here, and the rocks, at this hot spring weren't slippery. Not at all.

Unlike any hot spring remotely close to that awful Oakengal Academy.

Strange how the mist muted the sweet fun giggles of her girlfriends so well. She didn't recall the mist being so good at muting sound but then again she hadn't been here for years and years.

Least to her left, a few paces away, loomed a protective wall of scarlet ferns. Beyond it another boy barrier. Thorny rose vines weaved thickly through the waist-high green ferns. A shield against any accidental oopsies by stray boys of the human and dwarven kind.

But not a stray elf boy—or alf boy—doing some wicked woodrifting but so what?

Not many elf boys in these parts, well, except Ace and that cutie pie was the best kind of blendo boy to the extreme —elf, dwarf, and human all together—so no wicked woodrifting for him ... least hopefully not.

So yeah, safe to take a glance or few at herself and yay!

Her rosy-pink hair flowed as shiny cutesy as it could be straight down to the nap of her back. Only her slim bangs flowed down her front, and rested down along her breasts. Breasts all the artists for all her drawies said were the most heavenly endowed they ever well ... you know.

And between her legs no scales, so phewie yay!

As cutesy pink and silky soft as her scales were down there, when they dared showed themselves, right now it was just the toasted peachy complexion of her elven form as it should be, well, technically, of her alven form, but some secrets had to stay supersecret or else ...

Cringie was all too rightsie.

On the right side of the upper front of her hair was her precious hair clip, Heartzee. A gift from Ace, the cutest treasure ever from the cutest boy ever, from years ago. She never seen anything like it then or since and for good reason.

Not because it was shaped like cutesy fist-sized heart with a playful pink smile and even pinker, even cuter half-circle eyes.

But because Heartzee was actually some kind of living ... device, artifact, or something that—

"Oh Dazzle!" Heartzee said. "Ogle yourself much longer and—"

"And what?" Dazzle said. "I've got nothing to be ashamed of 💗 Lots to be proud of 💗 So hush ❣ Someone will hear you 💔 And that weird accent of yours—"

"As if!" Heartzee said. "I can barely hear you in this fog. There's magic muffling your voice. My voice. Everyone. We should be able to hear your girlfriends playing on the opposite side of the pool but do we? No. Just you kevchin'."

Kevching was her weirdo word for whining. (Probably for whining.)

Dazzle gulped. "Ravishing Ravager time, then 💔"

Normally Dazzle wouldn't hesitate so much but Leaflet was definitely nearby and Dazzle was an alf of the clawgirl kind so she had a second form that—

"Of course!" Heartzee said. "And don't worry. The eye mask will keep your identity concealed and perfectly at that. No magic can pierce it. None. Guaranteed or your money back."

"Money? You were a gift ♥" Dazzle said.

"And a great one at that!" Heartzee said. "Oy critics everywhere ... now don't forget you can sip a little blood as Ravager and you definitely need a sip or few. More than a little. Skin and bones, dearie, skin and bones, and this whole clawgirl thing you have going—"

Someone suddenly screamed. "Scum!"

A familiar truly-whiny someone. A horrible someone.

A wicked warlock who loved enslaving pretty girls for reasons stupid and creepy and ... so cringie it hurt just thinking of that scrawny whiny creep.

Dazzle gasped, quietly. Turn between running toward, or away from the scream.

"Warren Lock!" Dazzle said. "He's back!"

"Lock ... Lock ..." Heartzee said, "You mean a warlock of the Lock bloodline?"

"Yeah!" Dazzle said. "Before I got you. Warren ... he enslaved me, and all my elven girlfriends, and even some of my part-elf girlfriends like Zylah Bella, whose part succubus too."

"Oy," Heartzee said, "this is bad. That bloodline—"

"I know!" Dazzle said. "Ace only got Warren to free us last time by convincing Warren Ace would kill all of us—Warren, us slaved girls, and then himself."

"Wow that's ..." Heartzee said.

"Don't criticize him 🤍 🤍 🤍" Dazzle said. "Ace felt so guilty afterwards ... he got us all gifts as apologies🤍 You were mine and ..."

"Okay, okay," Heartzee said. "Maybe you're right. Don't go Ravager just yet. Use me as a fall back. And don't hesitate to—"

"To go clawgirl," Dazzle said, "without going clawgirl🤍 Yeah, yeah, I know🤍"

Clawgirls like Dazzle had plenty of natural fighting talents that improved not just with practice and experience but with age. In any form.

Alven or clawgirl.

She even could create and control pink lightning from her hands and feet—but only when she shifted them into claws. Segmented claws with eagle-like talons as pink as the lightning she could wield with them.

But to do that she'd need to shift her whole entire body too into her clawgirl form.

Her skin into snake-like scales of the vividly pink and super-protective kind (well not as protective between her breasts because reasons stupid and silly sounding.) Several couple-inch long spikes of the pale pink kind would poke out of the top of her pink hair. Teeth would go fanged cutesy. Eyes serpent slitted.

So as long as Dazzle didn't shift into her clawgirl form, as long as she went, as Ace called it, grasshopper gladiator, elf girl style ...

Heartzee moaned, but didn't comment this time.

"A dozen or so sprints straight forward," Heartzee said. "You can't miss him."

"Oh no 🩶 " Dazzle said. "That's where we left Leaflet 🩶 "

And so Dazzle took off. Sprinting as fast as she could.

Hoping beyond hope that Leaflet could hold out just a little bit longer.

CHAPTER 7
ACE DE SABER

That very instant. Ace. He felt Amber. Her warm amber flames embracing him from behind. Over his back. Over his arms. Flames as warm, as ticklish as a very warm cat's very tight cuddling.

Burning the nearest of the green ferns to ashy black. The thorny rose vines. Even a few roses.

Burning the blue fog back some. More then some. A few paces. More than a few paces.

No missing another whiff of peaches and cream with a sharp nip of fern. Of Leaflet once again. Why here? Now? If she was within, or near these ferns, she'd be thrown out already but …

Ack!

Amber. Her flame. She suddenly shove him down.

Rolling up him along the little dirt path.

Just as a bright violet blur swooped over him. A violet blur of claws and spikes.

No.

His eyes. They followed the blur.

Barely.

But they did.

That blur. Shaped too much like some attractive human girl but with light violet skin and covered here and there with violet snake scales—more like a bra top and bikini bottom of violet scales. Violet battish wings from between her shoulder blades. Wings wide enough to span her arms' length. A spiked lizard tail from the nap of her back.

And violet horns spiked out of the top of her waist-long pale-violet hair.

No. Not human girl.

A valkyrie vipress. A dragon. A very dangerous kind of human-like dragon.

Especially when on the wrong end of their flame and hate.

Like Ace was now—but why? Her big bright violet eyes held only rage and fury toward him.

Not terror. Not regret. Not even reluctance.

Ace rolled up to his feet.

Drew his sabers. Same time.

But didn't throw the slashes—or strengthen them into extralong and extrapowerful slices.

No.

Just as Amber whispered in his right ear again.

"I'll slip around behind her," Amber said. "You keep her distracted."

Scarlet then sighed in his left ear. "Going on ahead. See ya soon, sexy."

No need for him to say anything. Ace trusted both Amber and Scarlet to do what was necessary here. As genies Scarlet and Amber could, for some unknown reason, both slip into the shadows. Travel between connected shadows.

So slipping through the shadows underneath the roses and ferns. Amber going behind the vipress—and Scarlet even heading over to Warren ...

Purrfect as Amber would say. And Scarlet would actually add a real sensual purr to it.

So blades raised Ace growled at the valkyrie vipress.

"What's the meaning of this?" he said. "Did Warren slave you or—"

"Slave me?" the violet scaled girl said. "Is that what you humans call it?"

Several feet away from the tips of his sabers—but pointed at the big chest of hers despite the bright violet snake scales protecting the center and lower parts of it—and yet she merely tsked a huff.

Shoving her jiggling chest at him as if daring him to strike her through the chest.

That she hadn't attacked him again.

Yet.

Strange. This hesitation on her part.

"Where's your slave mark?" Ace said.. "Warren—"

She even then cocked her hips suggestively sideways, to

her right, right hand then resting on it. Her fingers segmented claws of bright solid violet so gleaming razor sharp Ace suspected they could slice through steel.

Including his own sabers.

Her left hand, within her segmented fingers, a pale violet ball of cackling flame.

"As if," she said, "I'm allowed to show you just because you asked."

True. Warren might have learned that lesson from last time.

Destroy the slave mark.

Destroy the spell controlling her and free her—unless her master would force her to kill herself upon release. And with Warren—

A light breeze in his face.

A sudden whiff of the sweet scent of grapes and ripe plums touched with vanilla?

"That scent," Ace said. "You're part elf."

Her ears sunk even more, but still jutted from the sides of her head like little few-inch long daggers.

Just like Leaflet's, or any other elf girl's.

"Of course," she said. "Only vipresses' with enough elf blood—like me—are worthy of my creepy master's attention."

Figures. How he caught her ...

"I'm Ace—"

She tsked again. "Ace de Saber. I *know*. That bastard won't shut up about you."

"You are?" Ace said.

"Does it matter?" she said. "Kill me while you can. I'm not worth saving."

Ace gnashed his teeth. Kill the vipress now and he might be able to save whoever Warren was attacking now but ... killing one of Warren's victims ... no, that was too much like Warren and his awful tricks. Too much like ... no. Just no.

Never!

But no sign of Amber yet either. What was taking her so long—

A yowl rang out next to the vipress? Paces to the right. From underneath the rose vines and ferns.

"Amber?" Ace said.

Just as those rose vines and ferns shuddered fiercely. A feline ack rang out.

"No!" Ace said. "Amber!"

But the vipress merely tsked at Ace again.

"A **genie**? Really?" the vipress said. "She dies—or I do."

And this time Ace. He ... he ...

CHAPTER 8
ROSALINE APPLEHART

The azure-blue fog was as dense as Rosaline Applehart was for thinking she could ever find her way back anywhere in it—let alone wherever she dumped all her clothing, her cute heart-shaped pouch alchemied to carry far too many things to lose all at once, and worst of all her brand new witch hat.

A witch hat that proved she's a true witch or something.

Least that she properly graduated from Oakengal Academy as a proper witch or something like that.

That witch hat was as lime green as her eyes (or so people have said.) Its brim. A few several inches wide. The left side slumped stylishly down and the right side stylishly up.

And of course, no witch hat was a real witch hat without an extra pointy crown.

And the tip of her hat's pointed crown coiled around and around and from its tip, dangling from a thin but secure inch-long chain of gold, was a polished-smooth emerald heart a whole sparkling couple inches big and framed securely in even shinier gold.

The perfect magical gem to store her excess mana—the energy used to fuel spells and magic in general—to use whenever she needed more than she had for spells and whatnot.

(Well, only while she actually wore the thing.)

Too bad that didn't work against regular fatigue, since wow, did she want to just sit down on one of these flat smooth boulders, with their soft blue moss cuddling her aching ass and even achier feet, and rest once again.

Walking all the way from Oakengal and not a touch of woodrifting to speed things up ... ugh, but Leaflet, Sky, and Starlite still kinda struggled to woodrift reliably so no telling where they'd end up if they tried to woodrift all the way here, or even near here.

At least the blue water of the hot spring was still a few feet to her left.

That water was stunningly smooth and clear. Even here. Not a single ripple. Despite all the boulders jutting out of the water. The blue moss over them dripping and dripping into the hot spring.

Stunningly reflective too. A lot like a spooky mirror.

Her bright scarlet hair ... scarecrow scary so ... some serious hand brushing and phew.

Now half flowed down wavy to the tips of her shoulder blades, the other half curled wavy over her right shoulder, and rested nice and cozy on her right breast.

And yeah ... maybe Dazzle was right. Rosaline was the most chestiest of them all, and the most hourglassy, and by far the most tasty to any monster out there.

Especially to any of those fake elves. Those elf-hunting alves.

Definitely especially to anything serpent or dragon or whatnot.

So good chance this Alitrooper crap will so get her killed in the worst way possible, or almost as bad, enslaved by some alf boy into (one of) his personal suck and fuck toys.

Unless Leaflet, Sky, and Dazzle manage to save her uselessly pretty ass again and again and again.

Maybe Starlite and Cellow would help out too. Occasionally.

So the spooky silence within this fog—despite her girlfriends all around her, or at least nearby, hopefully, too weird to risk singing to herself. Her voice always made weird things happen. Well, weirder things happen.

Except when she wanted it too—like with chants or incantations for spells.

(How she managed to graduate ... miracles do happen, sometimes.)

Sure the fog here in Mintwood muffled some sound but never this much. But then again she wasn't a woods guide like Ace so maybe it did get this bad naturally sometimes.

Yet that tingly feeling throughout her body ... especially tickling all over her all-too-bare skin ... too much like whenever she got dowsed in magical whatever, whether in class or especially in that awful dungeon full of monsters and mayhem.

Leaflet saved Rosaline and her uselessly pretty ass there more often than not.

Dazzle and Sky too.

Sometimes even Cellow and Starlite. Sometimes.

Lucky for Rosaline her three best girlfriends—Leaflet, Dazzle, and Sky—practically babysat her through those awful dungeon adventures. She only got nibbled on a few too many times and each time it was completely and utterly her own pathetically stupid fault.

To her left ... there should be a really high and thick wall of scarlet ferns but no, just blue fog too thick to see through now, so—

"Scum!"

That word. Screamed by the creepiest guy Rosaline ever had the mispleasure of being near, let alone a warlock that enslaved her years ago.

But that time, Ace de Saber, the bravest boy Rosaline ever met, saved her sorry ass. Even apologized for how he did so— despite not needing to but ... a gift was a gift and wow, did Ace know how to pick them.

A polished smooth ruby-red heart. A big sparkling inch big and framed in shiny silver—and not just a gemstone, but her first real magical gemstone.

A stone she still had—in her pouch.

(How he got it ... All Grandest connections and whatever.)

So Rosaline growled. Her mouth. Her throat tingling even more than usual.

"Warren Lock?" Rosaline said.

Stepping forward faster and faster and faster—until.

"Looking for thisss?"

Oh yay. A sinister serpent girl already found her next meal —Rosaline.

But a sinister serpent girl? Here? One of Warren's new slave girls then?

From the left too, so no escaping to the right, into the steaming hot spring.

Emerging from the thick fog where the scarlet ferns were supposed to be ... a tall graceful blonde blue-eyed wood elf girl strolled out. A girl wearing only a scarlet-snake-scaled bra top and bikini bottom and near where her shoulders blades would be were scarlet battish wings spanning out to her hands.

Hands and feet were ... segmented scarlet claws that gleamed extra sharp and ...

Oh crap. Not an elf girl of any sort. Least not anymore.

A valkyrie vipress. Those scarlet horns spiked out of the top of her head ... yeah.

Rosaline's done for—or slave time once again.

Since in that serpent girl's hands—Rosaline's precious lime-green witch hat.

CHAPTER 9
ACE DE SABER

Ace ... He ... He ... no.

A deep calming breath full of fragrant rose, grapish elf girl musk, and worst of all, peaches and cream nipped bitter with fear—Leaflet was in trouble and Warren, that wretched warlock ...

No. Focus. Calm.

As calm as the gentle breeze. As solid as the fog thickening around them.

And as burning fierce as the muggy heat.

Good. Grounded. As grounded as this dirt path.

What would Uncle Hammer do in this situation?

This little dirt path gave no maneuver room. On each side the green ferns and the rose vines tangling through them. No passing through them. Not without the ability to woodrift, or travel through shadow, or something Ace had no ability to do.

Treat them as hazards. Wallish hazards. Nothing more.

Retreat wasn't an option. Ahead the path rose higher. Behind the path fell lower.

Only feet ahead of him and that violet valkyrie vipress had the upper ground. Several inches on him, actually, despite being near the same height, and her left hand already held a ball of violet flame to throw at him.

Ace. His steel sabers were out and pointed right between her breasts. Stab her there and, if his readings of All Grandest teachings were correct about her kind, she'd suffer a slow and agonizing death, but grow weaker immediately, so even if she fought back, the fight would be all but lost for her.

The deep dark shadow to the right a few feet away. The spot that shuddered the ferns and thorny rose vines. The place where Amber cried out in pain and seemed to be trapped … somehow.

"So …" Ace said, "a suicidal vipress? Really? Where's your pride?"

The vipress tsked even more scornfully.

"Gone," she said, "with my freedom."

"So better dead," Ace said, "then thralled."

"Exactly," she said. "Just make it quick. As quick as you can. Hurry. Before he catches on."

Yet Ace. He hesitated. Again.

Easy kill and he'd save Amber, and then Leaflet, and help Scarlet, but …

Deep down. Ice. Ice seemed to tingle down his spine. Goosebump his arms.

Despite the muggy heat.

Not saving this vipress ... wait. What if this was a trap? A scheme.

A strange scheme but a scheme.

That look in her violet eyes. All that scorn toward Ace. Unlike Dazzle and Sky, unlike Rosaline and Leaflet years ago, back when Warren slaved them all, the fear and reluctance in their eyes was unmistakable.

Something was off. Dangerously off.

But what?

A hunch. Merely a hunch but this vipress and shadows ...

What if she had some power connected to the shadows? Amber shouted in his ear about the shadows a moment before this vipress attacked him.

And Uncle Hammer drilled into him to trust that instinct, especially in a fight—that instinct sensed things Ace himself didn't notice so ...

So Ace flung his right-handed saber straight at the deep dark shadow to the right of the vipress. At the shadow underneath the green ferns and rose vines. The shadow from where Amber cried out. Make the plants all shudder.

Or so it seemed to be Amber.

Since the moment the saber pierced the shadows—the cry wasn't Amber's voice this time.

It was the vipress'.

CHAPTER 10
ACE DE SABER

That very instant the vipress before Ace shattered into violet flame and ash.

Just as the ferns and vines a few feet to the right shuddered even more violently this time, and didn't stop shuddering now. Just like how the moans and groans from that spot. From that devious vipress.

Moment before that violet flame vanished before him.

Revealing it was Amber that had been mere feet before him …

That truly gorgeous golden-haired blue-eyed human-like girl but with big pointed cat ears from the sides of her head, a long cat tail from the nap of her back, and big and furry hands and feet of the pawishly cute cat kind.

Amber had amber tiger-like fur with dark-black suggestive stripes covering her around her colossally cute chest and heavenly hips, kinda like a two-piece bikini, but was real genuine fur growing out of her.

Just like the ball of amber flame dancing from the tips of her cat ears and the tip of her tail.

Her eyes. Blink. Blink. Blink.

And she gasped.

"Ace?!" Amber said. "I. I. I."

With his free hand Ace grabbed both of her furry soft pawish hands.

"You're alright," Ace said. "That's what matters."

And he gave her a tender squeeze.

"Oh Ace ..." Amber said.

Then she jolted in place. "Oh no. No time. Scarlet!"

"Exactly," Ace said. "Be my second saber."

Amber purred. "My pawleasure!"

Ah. Amber always loved adding paw and purr and other kitty words into how she spoke.

Scarlet too.

They called it talking kitty style and Ace couldn't help but like it too.

An instant later Amber bursted into amber flames and then, giggling out loud all cutesy and happy, those flames flew swirling into Ace's right hand, where, a moment later, instead of a steel saber in his right hand, he held a completely different saber.

A truly magical one.

One with a slightly curved thin blade of roiling amber flames restrained by tiger-like dark-stripes coiled around the amber flame.

The hilt. Two tiger paws. Claws out.

Fierce and facing the same direction as the tip of the blade.

And the handle—as soft and cozy as the pads on Amber's pawish hands.

The balance. As light as a feather.

Its strength. As powerful as dragon flame—if not more.

Amber giggled happy as ever.

"Time to wreck that wicked Warren," Amber said, "now and pawever more!"

But Ace didn't need to respond with words.

He responded with action.

With a single fiery slash Ace burned a path through the ferns and vines. A path straight up to that scream.

CHAPTER II
DAZZLE SPARKLES

Dazzle dashed and dashed faster and faster as straight as she could into the deep-blue mist. The blue moss thick on the ground. Her bare feet slammed into it. Not slipping. Not one bit.

Each and every sprint.

The muggy hot air, mist flushed against her bare skin. Like swimming through mint-spiced steam.

But still too slowly.

Far too slowly.

Warren hadn't needed much time last time he enslaved Dazzle and her girlfriends. Even without ambushing them. Without the element of surprise.

No chance Leaflet could fend Warren off completely by herself. Not for long.

Not unarmed.

A sudden whiff of Leaflet's peaches and cream musk

carried by the breeze, the humid breeze, too much like breathing peaches and cream juice …

But with a bitter touch of fear to it.

Part of it excited Dazzle. Her sinister clawgirl side. The side that yearned to feed on the flesh and blood of elves, of humans, of dwarves.

Part of it terrified Dazzle. Her other side—whatever her other side was … elven? Her father was an elf, after all, but mother was clawgirl and so …

No!

Focus!

Dash straight!

Straight! Straight! Straight!

Sprint! Sprint! Sprint!

Leaflet! Dazzle must save poor dear Leaflet! No one else here could—

The roiling thick mist pulled back very suddenly. Revealing more moss-covered ground.

Empty ground.

Lumps and rocks but not a hint of Leaflet. Of damaged moss from a struggle. Or even a bootprint from Warren, or clawprint from whatever creatures he brought with him.

Just as blink. From behind her. Trinkling so softly. Almost silent.

Almost.

A stream of flying water—a solid tube of clear azure-blue water a couple feet wide—coiled around and around her?!

A gasp.

Its steam. Scented with a strange spearmint—sharper than the mint-scented fog.

But no stopping now!

Dazzle was faster—barely.

From her sprint she leapt. Somersaulting over the coils of steaming water.

And into the coils of another stream of steaming blue water?!

Water than encased her an instant later. Scolding her awfully. Shoving itself into her mouth. Her nose. Into her deeper and deeper. More and more painful. Drowning without hope.

Her breath.

Gone.

Her body. Staining to move. Unable to move. Strangled. As if the water was a serpent itself. Squeezing the life out of her.

Cackles erupted from within the water? Wicked girl cackles.

"Another pet elf captured," the wicked girl-voice said, "and one boy to go!"

No! Never! Ace. Leaflet. Rosaline. Sky.

But how to escape …. Heartzee couldn't help unless she could move and activate her so …

Clawgirl time.

A bestie was a bestie. Saving Leaflet—even if Dazzle herself was banished for being a clawgirl—no regrets!

Yupsie!

No regrets.

So Dazzle shifted right there and then into her clawgirl form. Done in an instant.

An instant as if relaxing a muscle throughout her own body.

Her skin. It felt like it stretched out in place—turning to snake-like scales of the wonderfully vivid pink and protective kind. Her eyes stretched too. Pupils into slits. Teeth tugged into fangs.

And best of all her hands and feet hardened, stretched out, and fused together. All in that instant.

Into eagle-like claws. Talons cackling with wonderfully pink lighting.

Lightning shocking the entire glop of water around Dazzle. Even tingling Dazzle through her scales.

But just tingling.

The wicked girl-voice shrieked. "No! A clawgirl! But-But-But!"

Dazzle gasped. Water flushing out of her.

"Yes!" Dazzle said. "Clawgirl extraordinaire! Here to save my besties—"

The water glop around Dazzle exploded. Tingling vanishing that instant.

A thump behind Dazzle.

Moans.

"Damn ... you ... traitor," the wicked girl-voice said. "When I recover ... Storm Talonwind shall be your death. If Warren doesn't ... doesn't ... damn you. Die and ..."

Dazzle glanced back at her fallen foe, Storm whatever ... a lovely-looking valkyrie vipress?

Yeah. Collapsed and nearly unconscious on the ground.

Blue scaled undies-in-public kind of appearance. Usual battish wings from her shoulder blades spanning her arms' length. Horns poking out of the top of her short shoulder-length pale blue hair.

"Die?" Dazzle said. "You first😈"

And from both her clawed hands Dazzle blasted a bolt of pink lightning at the valkyrie vipress. At her most vulnerable spot—the same spot as Dazzle had—between her breasts and boom!

Gasp. Shocked at the obvious.

But now no more Storm whatever to worry about.

Time to save not just Leaflet, Sky, and Rosaline—but Ace too!

But as an elf girl once again (or so Dazzle hoped.)

CHAPTER 12
ROSALINE APPLEHART

Better play dumb. Yeah. Really dumb.

Ravishing redhead dumb.

Rosaline was ravishingly beautiful enough for people to believe her stupid dumb act completely—whether it really was an act or not—and good thing too. Master Hammer said all the time getting underestimated was far better than overestimated, least in a fight, so ...

Wait. Oh no no no.

Master Hammer also said to pay attention to what's around her. Just in case she could use it in the fight—or avoid it being used against her.

But the fog already started closing back in. Only steps away, at the edge before the fog ahead of Rosaline, was that scarlet-scaled blonde valkyrie vipress.

Only smooth lumps of blue moss between them. And the empty muggy hot air.

Far too close for Rosaline to chant a spell—even a one-word quickie. Forget reciting an entire incantation.

As powerful as those incantations were they were always so, so slow because of how many words she had to incantate, which was a fancy word for speak while mixing her mana with the words at the right levels at the right moments and so on and so forth.

The mint-smell of the fog. Stronger than ever.

Why ... Rosaline had no idea. Never did. She didn't even realize before her time as Oakengal that fog elsewhere didn't smell like mint.

But now there was that apple and peaches smell from the vipress—despite the strong mint smell of the fog ... which meant she was part elf girl so ... she'd yearn even more for elf girl flesh and blood. More than valkyrie vipresses without elf girl in them.

Rosaline nibbled her lower lip. That stupid cherry and apple taste. From herself.

No.

Excitement. Not fear.

Fear only would make her tastier to this vipress.

So don't worry about how the fog was slowly but steadily closing in beside her.

Much.

Even if the vipress held Rosaline's precious lime-green witch hat. Rosaline's only hope for a future. A real future. One where she'd be able to cast powerful spells and incantations and and and maybe survive her Alitrooper duties that ...

Oh crap.

This very fight. Too much like what she'd need to do over and over and over and ...

So better get used to coming up with trick and traps or else slave girl munchie time.

Do what she knew best. Least this time. Before the fog swallowed them both.

Swallowed them and who knew what would happen then?

So cocking her hips sexy sideways Rosaline imagined the vipress held the most precious magical gemstone ever—even better than her witch hat's, the very best, the Emerald of the End or something—and just for Rosaline.

The very thought. Yeah! It lit Rosaline up. Her mana tingled throughout her whole entire all-too-nude body. No doubt her expression was now as excited and happy and as believable as possible.

"Oh, wow, yeah!" Rosaline said. "Thanks!"

Despite her heart racing faster than a mouse from a cat, no, her kitty cat Diddles loved playing with mice, with anything, befriending anything small or large, unlike most cats, so giggle giggle.

Yeah.

Giggle giggle. All sultry sweet and stupid and clueless.

So stupid and clueless she best ignore how the fog now roiled spooky angrily around them.

So Rosaline strutted closer and closer to the valkyrie vipress. No hesitation either.

Embrace her inner Diddles.

Yeah. Diddles.

Instead of a playful purr and meow Rosaline let out a sultry happy giggle or two. To break the eerie silence. Silence made by the fog. Ignore the fog closing in more and more. Only a couple steps to her sides now. Ready to swallow them both.

Blind Rosaline and the silence—silence her magic too.

The vipress blinked at Rosaline. Only a couple steps away and the vipress growled.

"Are you really *that* stupid?!" the vipress said. "This hat is **mine** now!"

A moment later. Another step close.

And that hat now within reach of Rosaline's hands too—but no. Not yet.

Embrace her inner Diddles. Yeah.

Diddles.

But the fog. That solid-seeming azure-blue wall edged so close. She didn't dare spread her arms out, close. No telling what was inside that fog.

Waiting.

But no. Not even her toes dared grip the moss tighter.

No. Savor the soft moss between her bare-naked toes. Yeah.

Since annoying this vipress stupid ... as stupid as Rosaline was acting, kinda like how Dazzle went super ditzy to annoy her rivals into making stupid mistakes, especially her girl rivals ... now that's Rosaline's only hope to overcome this vipress.

So Rosaline tsked. As if this was just a friendly spat. Then settled in a standing cocked sexy to the side pose.

"Well we're both naked here—" Rosaline said.

"What does that have to do with anything?" the vipress said. "Your cherry and apple stink should be bittersweet with fear, not so stupidly sweet!"

Good. Embracing her inner Diddles was working wonders. No fear.

Just stupidly happy.

"Ooo," Rosaline said, "an apple and peaches girl! Great combo for—"

The vipress slapped Rosaline across her cheeks. Those segmented claws. They ripped through her cheeks. Through her mouth.

Ripping part of Rosaline's face off.

Rosaline gasped. Air coming, escaping where it shouldn't.

While the pain. The agony.

It made Rosaline wobbled on her feet. This vipress. Too much like those monsters in the dungeon at Oakengal. Monsters Leaflet and Dazzle and Sky saved Rosaline from all the time.

But no one would save Rosaline here. Not this time. Especially not once Rosaline started that Alitrooper duties with everyone else. No telling how long they'd be allowed to watch Rosaline's back.

Least her own regenerative healing restored her cheeks and mouth quickly, already. Only leaving aches. Really, really awful aches.

But Diddles. He didn't have healing like Rosaline.

So how did he manage to stay so carefree and friendly?

The vipress chuckled, all hissy and horrible. Too much like a monster herself.

Then the vipress slapped Rosaline across her cheeks against. In the opposite direction. Ripping her cheeks and mouth off again.

Rosaline yowled in agony.

Dropped to her knees.

Bang!

The rock underneath the moss. Too hard. Too solid.

Too painful.

"Looks like," the vipress said, "I'll have to torment you for the right flavor—"

Rosaline clenched her teeth. Her cheeks. They ... they already knitted themselves back together. Her mouth restored itself. Quickly and completely.

As a wood elf Rosaline could heal so fast and quickly and ... just gotta ... gotta ...

The vipress had some of Rosaline's ... bloody cheek dangling from her claws.

Until the vipress slurped it all down.

"Now," the vipress said, "for your breasts. The tastiest part too!"

Before Rosaline could shove herself away the vipress swiped her segmented claws at Rosaline. At her chest and ack.

Stars.

Pain.

Breath. Gone.

From pain.

Trembling her body.

And yet. Deep down. Not just a desire to live. No. More.

Rage. Fury.

Bad enough this vipress was ripping Rosaline into a meal one swipe at a time. This awful vipress also had somehow tossed aside Rosaline's precious lime-green witch hat as if it was nothing at all—and Rosaline hadn't even noticed until now.

That. That. At how ... how ... that was it.

Rosaline snarled.

"Drop dead you bitch!" Rosaline said. "And here I thought we could be friends—"

The act. Rosaline couldn't make herself drop the act now.

Even if she rejected her inner Diddles now.

The vipress slapped Rosaline cross her cheeks again. Ripping through them and then slurping up the rest.

"Friends?" the vipress said. "Ha! Do cats befriend their mice? No! They ... they ..."

Rosaline tried to respond. Her cheeks, Her chest. They had healed already but the tingling in her throat. Deep within her pained aching chest.

"My little Diddles loves playing with mice!" Rosaline said. "As **friends!**"

"Ha! Stupid thing!" the vipress said. "That ... that ... what the ..."

The vipress dropped to her knees. "Impossible. An insta-death spell?! When?!?!?"

What the ...

But the hazing of the vipress' eyes. The strain in her body all of a shudder.

The fog roiling around them. No right at the tips of Rosaline's elbows but no longer coming closer.

No.

It slowly but steadily pulled back. More and more.

As if the fog closing in was the vipress' fault.

Just as … as … Rosaline. Her voice. All that tingling in her mouth, her throat, even deep within her, where her breath came from … impossible but …yeah, that hazing over of the vipress' eyes. Still getting worse and worse for her.

Her trembling shock.

Just like the last time Rosaline used a insta-death spell like that one. On a monster. A very vicious and sadistic monster in that dungeon underneath Oakengal.

The tingling throughout Rosaline. Her whole mouth. Her throat. Deep inside her. Where her breath came from. It hadn't even faded. No. But settled down. As if …. If her mana, her mana was flowing there naturally, not forced through her own will like casting a chant and incantation.

Could maybe …

"Yeah," Rosaline said. "An insta-death spell. Your turn to die. So go die!"

"But … but … your hat," the vipress said. "No chant. No incantation. No wand or staff! So how …"

"My voice is magic, bitch!" Rosaline said.

And with all her strength Rosaline slapped the vipress across her cheeks.

Hard.

Hard enough to really hurt herself—but so what? Rosaline recovered even quicker.

Unlike the vipress.

The vipress toppled over. Crashing to the ground.

Already dead.

Rosaline's precious witch hat right beside the dead vipress' unmoving head.

CHAPTER 13

LEAFLET PEACHES

Leaflet. Her gasp. Not. Not her last but but but …

The sharp pain through up through her back, into her heart. Her body trembled. Standing there. Clamped there on the mossy ground. Trembling before that creepy warlock Warren. The mist closing in more and more.

The moments of eerie silence.

Not a giggle or splash from her girlfriends in the distance. From across the spring.

And yet the way that warlock screamed scum … not even the mist dared muffle it. As if … if Warren wanted everyone to know Leaflet was mere scum, all for not being this warlock's braindead devoted slave.

And the mist, over the pool, faded the mossy boulders into azure blue, it started roiling, roiling like storm clouds, and getting thicker and thicker, the once smooth flat water …

Now tainted with ripples. Lots and lots and ripples.

Silent ripples.

All from Warren screaming the word "scum."

Rosaline sometimes could do something like that. Her voice had magic in it but not like Warren there. Rosaline and her magical voice never did much beyond affect feelings, or shake everything up a little bit, or or or …

Warren was clamping his clammy hand down on Leaflet's left shoulder even harder. As if sucking something out of Leaflet too. Her strength? Her stamin? What?

Her body trembled. Shivered from exhaustion?

No! Not now!

She'd never see Ace again—after all this time and she was so close … her girlfriends. They were next! Leaflet had to stop Warren. Stop him here and now.

Somehow …

Leaflet could only do what Master Hammer suggested as a last resort.

"Oh how noble," Leaflet said, "you are to sneak up on a naked girl and stab her in the back. How really, really noble of you."

Warren snarled. "You're born scum. I'm born nobility! Now die! Die die die!"

Leaflet felt him wrench, twist the dagger he had plunged up into her back. All while tightening his clammy grip on her shoulder. Her feet. They somehow managed to keep their grip on the soft blue moss. Despite her legs wobbling more and more.

"You first!" Leaflet said.

And her right elbow. Still free and now, with all her

might, she shoved through whatever Warren did to slow her down. Shoving her elbow toward the side of his midriff and —ack!

Her knees. One after the other. Pain jolted, kicked them forward. No. Warren kicked her knees from behind! her feet. They didn't slid but ...

Leaflet fell, forced down onto her knees.

Just as Warren shoved Leaflet down further—using that awful dagger and his hand together.

Her face. The moss. Its mint scent was all too strong. Stabbingly strong. With each breath. Strained breath.

But no resisting Warren. He was shoving her face right deep into the blue moss. The taste of the moss. Like rough minty salad of the rawest and most sour kind.

Then. Even harder. Against the stone underneath the moss.

Hard against.

"No," Warren said, "**you** first, bitch."

"Ace," Leaflet said. "He'll avenge me. Us. Just you wait."

"I'm counting on it," Warren said, "And you, my dear monster minion to be, will be there to betray and butcher him with your own little stupid hands!"

"Never!" Leaflet said. "I'd never ... I'd rather die than ... than ..."

"As if," Warren said, "you'll have a choice. I don't need alven blood to slave you to my cause. I'm a warlock of the noble Lock bloodline! I can bind you all to me and—"

A fiery boom erupted paces behind them. Near the scarlet ferns!

The smell of roasted fern. A wave of extra hot heat. A strong breeze of even hotter air.

Just as everything shook wildly. So wildly her face.

Her face slammed several times into the mossy ground. Bang. Bang. Bang. By Warren shaking as well. The ground shaking too. The moss softening the blows but not by much. Not by enough. Her healing kicked in quickly and saved her from serious damage.

But his clampy hand. Its gripe was looser. Far looser.

The dagger in her back. No longer digging in as deeply.

Now!

Now was her chance to escape!

CHAPTER 14
WARREN LOCK

Warren. The world. Everything suddenly shook. Shook with that horribly loud boom behind him. That gust of hot air. Air stinking of burnt fern. Right from where he had slipped through that wall of red ferns. Through that wall and ran into his first target—Leaflet Peaches.

But now. Now his hands. They were jolting with the rest of him.

His grip. Looser and looser—and far too soon!

But this. This had to be some spell. A spell he could throw off and—

The lap of water. That sound. The splash of water against rocky shoreline. Against boulders here and there. No! Everything should be silent. Eerie silence. No magic except his own and his wives'. Nothing more. Nothing leas.

But this shaking. It really was all from that boom. That explosion.

Not some spell shocking him.

But no.

His wife Storm! What was she doing? The fog should be thicker. Muting even this boom. Reducing its power to nothing. Physical and magical power nullified—should be nullified. What the ...

"WARREN!!!"

That roar. That furious voice. A guy he recognized and yet couldn't recognize?!

The tingling in his ears. Magic. Magic was shielding the identity of that voice.

Somehow.

Despite his own magical powers to counter any such pathetic spells.

So Warren turned toward the voice. Without thinking he turned. His heart leaping to his throat.

The wall of red ferns.

Gone.

Roasted away by some kind of amber flame spell. A massive flame-natured spell.

In its place ... on the ashy flaming ground a terrifying monster?

Like a guy but dressed in a sinister jester outfit. A wiry guy no taller than five foot eight but that hat. Like two floppy horns with jiggling balls of gold at the ends. The red and yellow stars, hearts, and stripes all over his shirt and slacks.

But that whole entire outfit wasn't clothing in the usual sense.

No.

It was all roiling flames. Flames that even consumed the moss that jester stepped on as he marched toward Warren.

The stink of feline? Of mint and vanilla? Of … of … what the?

Such stinks didn't match a jester monster at all.

Unless … Warren's heard of such a creature before … somewhere …

Since in the jester's left hand—a saber of amber flame with black tiger-like stripes around the flames, as if constraining those amber flames.

Warren gasped. Then snarled.

"Phantom Jester?! I'm no bandit you—"

"You're worse!" the Phantom Jester said. "A savage slaver abducting innocent girls!"

"Curse you!" Warren said. "These elves are peasant scum. They're my rightful loot!"

Suddenly Leaflet jolted out of his grip? Rolling away. To the right.

But his dagger—it was still lodged in her back. Deep in her back. In her heart.

Only a matter of time before she crumbles to green sparkles. Those sparkles get sucked into the dagger and the dagger yes!

Just delay delay delay and the victory shall be his. A silent chant needed a few moments and no more.

Quick and deadly ice lightning should do the trick. End that fiery menace of a jester monster.

Then victory was his. Warren Lock's. The rightful heir of the noble Lock bloodline!

CHAPTER 15
ACE DE SABER

The poor moss roasted into ash quickly underneath his feet but as the Phantom Jester Ace had no better choice than to trigger the hottest, most protective of his flames—no telling what spells and incantations Warren would throw at Ace while he struck as the Phantom Jester.

The fog had retreated several paces. Roiling backwards. Revealing plenty of lumps of blue moss. Empty hot air.

But also plenty of space to fight in the open.

Even better Warren was near the edge of the pool.

The azure-blue water rippled like crazy. Unlike its usual calm and smoothly flat self. Lapping loud and clear against the shoreline. Splashing here and there too. Very unusual.

And Leaflet—thanks to Scarlet's advice and Phantom Jester's dramatic entrance only moments ago—Leaflet managed to slip out of that warlock's grip.

Roll to the right. Roll away from him. A pace or so to the right.

But that dagger. Still in her back. Up between her shoulder blades and ... oh no.

A heart strike from behind!

Had she been human, or even only part elf, she would certainly be dead, but as a full pure-blooded elf who trained under Uncle Hammer personally, she definitely could hold on a little longer.

But not too much longer.

Only a pace to the right Leaflet had collapsed from the roll onto her face. Clearly struggling to breath now. Her ass-long golden hair covering her mostly and jokes about hair being ass-long aside ...

No time to chit chat. Not at all. He already wasted too much time.

Phantom Jester snarled at Warren.

"Prepare to die this time," Phantom Jester said. "No mercy to wicked warlock scum!"

That scrawny creep. Paces in front of Phantom Jester. Unarmed but not helpless Warren wore a robe of scarlet snake scales that gleamed and—no.

Dragon scales.

Just as Scarlet had warned Ace. Scales that could absorb most physical and magical attacks.

Enhance the warlock's magical attacks as well.

Warren screamed. The rage in those dark eyes, so what?

"Next time!" Warren said. "Next time you'll die with them all!"

Phantom Jester's rage. It exceeded well beyond that warlock's. Enough rage to power the most fiery slash Phantom Jester could muster.

To lunge with that slash.

Warren waved his arms. A wall of thick solid azure blue ice rose up between them.

"I know who you are Jester!" Warren said. "I'll hunt you down and kill you."

But the Phantom Jester lunged.

Faster than a blink of a human eye.

Faster than even Uncle Hammer and his faster maneuvers.

Faster than any silent death chant Warren might try.

Warren snarled. Foolishly standing his ground.

"Kill everyone you ever cared for!" Warren said.

The wall of ice melted like snow against an inferno.

Warren screamed again. Hands, palms at Jester. Blue lightning cackling around them.

Jester midair—no way to dodge. Counter.

"Lightning of Iced Hell!!!" Warren said.

The blue lightning cackled like ice and electric between his hands.

It zigzagged toward Jester. And Jester couldn't even maneuver his sword to block it.

Not this close.

Not this fast.

But he didn't need to.

Another sword cut Warren down now even faster. A saber with a pink blade. It sliced through his wrists—where the scarlet scales didn't cover the warlock. A slice that cauterized the wounds instantly. A blade that had to belong to the legendary Ravishing Ravager.

Warren's gasp. Shock.

Snarl.

The wrong reaction.

A second pink-bladed saber sliced through his neck.

Just as flame suddenly engulfed Warren. A whirlwind of scarlet and pink flame. Roaring and screaming louder than Warren in life.

Nothing could survive that infernal column of whirling flame.

Nothing.

Not even the Phantom Jester.

Warren had to be dead and gone. Finally.

"Till next time, my sweet Jester 🤍🤍🤍" the Ravishing Ravager said.

Another giggle and the Ravishing Ravager was gone too—before Jester could even get a look at her. Let alone land on the ground.

Just like how Leaflet was safe—the dagger no longer in her back.

Good. The nightmare was over.

Like all mysterious heroes—time to vanish into the mist.

CHAPTER 16
LEAFLET PEACHES

Leaflet jolted awake ... to a cackling bonfire?

Yeah.

Like a spiky mountain of orange flame licking the dark night sky above, and before her. Lightning up the darkness all around them with its warmth nice and invigorating heat and constant cackles ... but the lumps of blue moss all around her ... the smell of mossy mint ... the gentle lap of water nearby ... as if ... she was still near the hot spring, near Cool Crater Pool.

So was that Warren thing just a nightmare or ... no.

The ache in her back. The sharp ache in her heart. The sudden strain in her breath.

Side-effects of recovering from such a terrible wound.

So ... it wasn't a dream but ... the thick blue moss felt nice and comfy underneath her ... better than some mattresses in those inns Leaflet and her girlfriends stayed in on the way back from Oakengal Academy.

Still. She was bare naked. Unlike her time at any of those inns.

Blue moss meant she definitely was still close to Cool Crater Pool. The lapping water was the hot spring in some way. As quiet as it usually was there. Something still disturbed the water some, but so what?

If it was dangerous she would already be dead—or in worse trouble.

But crickets and frogs chirped and burped. All loud and louder. Nothing holding them back. More than enough to confirm she was safe. No trouble nearby.

Least for the moment.

And the moss here wasn't quite as wet as before but now, so very soft and silky cozy. Perfect for another good nap or even more sleep. A sigh and just maybe she would go back to sleep but ... what happened to everyone? She ... how could Leaflet sleep while everyone ... she didn't even know what happened to everyone.

How selfish of her. That ... that ... wait.

A cloak over her? Yeah. A green cloak. Like a cozy blanket.

A dry blanket.

In its middle was a five-leafed lime-green clover—each leaf about a foot wide—and with braided vines of real shiny gold around the whole clover. The emblem of not just the Alicorned Ones but of Alitroopers in general?

But ... an Alitrooper cloak? Here? Wait ...

Yeah. Her upcoming duties as an Alitrooper and ... they all

did carry some Alitrooper things from Oakengal. They had permission to go home to Greensap Village first. Visit family and friends for a few days at least before saying so long once again and ... gulp.

A familiar giggle next to her. A slim hand gently patted her head. Like Leaflet was a little kidlet again.

And that familiar whiff of strawberries and cream.

"Dazzle?" Leaflet said. "Wha ... what happened? I ... Warren but."

"No worries," Dazzle said. "Warren's gone and he won't be coming back."

"But ..." Leaflet said.

She gazed at the bonfire. Gone? Warren ... then he was dead? Somehow.

But how?

"No butts," Dazzle said, "except yours resting here and now🩶 The others went for help at Greensap🩶 It's close by so they should return soon enough🩶"

"But Dazzle—" Leaflet said.

Dazzle giggled playfully. Not letting up on the hand petting.

"I'll be captain of our team," Dazzle said, "so better get used to listening to me, he-he🩶"

Dazzle was right, sortof. She would be captain. She was the best fighter among them. Even Cellow, that martial arts geek admitted that much. The others just as much. Even Leaflet.

"Fiiiiine," Leaflet said. "Do you ... you save me?"

"Tell you later🤍 " Dazzle said. "Just go sleepy poo for now🤍"

Leaflet sighed. "Then ... maybe Ace will ..."

"Yup❣" Dazzle said. "Ace is definitely coming tonight. What other woods guide would come for us now, at night? So better rest up❣ I'll wake you when he arrives."

Leaflet cuddled herself. Happy to be alive, still, and hoping beyond hope that this time, Ace would be the one to save them, today, no, tonight.

He wanted to be a hero after all. Time to save the damsels in distress.

Just like they did in kidlet games so long ago.

A rustle of leaves behind Leaflet and the familiar scent of mint and vanilla—and not from Sky but from ...

Ace chuckled like the clueless cute fool he was.

"Nice night for a camp-out," he said. "Mind if I join in?"

And finally Leaflet felt she was safe and sound again— and home.

About the Author

Widely traveled, Jonathan Evan Hudson spends as much time studying life as he does writing gripping tales of fantastic adventures. From the giant redwoods of California to the deserts of Israel, his thrilling stories all draw on first-hand experiences and expand them with the fantastic and his acclaimed creativity.

Be the first to know!
For the updates and more:
www.JonathanEvanHudson.com

youtube.com/@jonathanevanhudson
tiktok.com/@jonathan.evan.hudson

A War Of Lust And Oak

Read Now!

✝ The Elf Girl Effect

Read Now!

The acclaimed Jonathan Evan Hudson once again weaves an unforgettable tale brimming with spicy page-turning action and fast-burning enemies-to-lovers passion.

Meet the newly knighted Roo Vorshaya. Sworn to protect humanity in the isolated mountain town of Appleharth. Dreams of action-packed adventure and passionate love under a lovely but sinister strawberry-pink sky.

Love re-ignited by a whiff of the familiar peaches and cream scent of his long-lost childhood girlfriend: the notorious elven witch Amber Peaches.

And endangering everything Roo holds dear.

Love page-turner novels of epic fantasy? Love reading from dusk to dawn? Then go read *The Elf Girl Effect* now!

Martial Art Of The Phantom Saber

Read Now!

Succubus Slash

Read Now!

The acclaimed Jonathan Evan Hudson weaves an unforgettable tale of thrilling action and adventure spiced with fast-burning romance and doused deep in epic fantasy.

Enter Miles Mayhem. Rich in friends and enemies. And a fat boy badass in the sword.

A seriously delicious smell of bacon and eggs smothered in spiced razor-hot cheddar signals celebration—and serious trouble ahead.

Trouble beyond anything Miles ever expected.

The perfect epic fantasy novel. A genre-enlarging feast for fans of sexy action and fabulous adventure. Read *Succubus Slash* now!

Sword Master Of Honey Heart Resort

Read Now!

Into Shadow Forest

Read Now!

A diamond in the rough the bestselling Jonathan Evan Hudson weaves a thrilling tale from explosive beginning to satisfying end in the awe-inspiring land of Grandcrest.

The talented twenty-something sword master Romeo Bladell yearns for love and adventure.

And at the musty edges of Shadow Forest. Near the towering high oaks bearded like stout old dwarves. By a canyon like a wound gnashed deep through in the granite. A canyon like the maw of a stone dragon.

A strange unexpected rope bridge hangs silently. Sinisterly.

Beckoning adventure—and danger unimaginable.

Enter *Into Shadow Forest* and savor the most spectacular of page-turning epic fantasy novels. Love unique monsters, riveting battles, and fantastic femme fatales? Then read *Into Shadow Forest* now!

Angels Of The Sword

Read Now!

Crossing Of Shadowed Death

Read Now!

The acclaimed master of fantasy Jonathan Evan Hudson once again shines through with his talented story-telling. Time to enter another stunning awe-inspiring world of dangerous demons, magical mayhem, and action-packed adventure.

A simple demon-hunting mission. The young and lonely Dirk yearns for amazing adventure, for gorgeously under-dressed dancer girls among the towering high ferns. Among the even taller pines of the hot and humid Fern Shadow Forest.

Pine needles everywhere. And so fragrant they made the finest of teas.

Sturdy reliable cobble roads of the Divine Empire cut through the whole entire forest. Providing the only safe passage.

Or so Dirk thought ...

Enjoy this sexy, action-packed epic fantasy adventure from the talented Jonathan Evan Hudson. Love to read an enthralling epic fantasy novel full of stunning rip-roaring battles with creative new monsters? Then go read *Crossing of Shadowed Death* now!

A TASTE OF SUCCUBUS SLASH

The acclaimed Jonathan Evan Hudson weaves an unforgettable tale of thrilling action and adventure spiced with fast-burning romance and doused deep in epic fantasy.

Enter Miles Mayhem. Rich in friends and enemies. And a fat boy badass in the sword.

A seriously delicious smell of bacon and eggs smothered in spiced razor-hot cheddar signals celebration—and serious trouble ahead.

Trouble beyond anything Miles ever expected.

The perfect epic fantasy novel. A genre-enlarging feast for fans of sexy action and fabulous adventure. Read **Succubus Slash** *now!*

CHAPTER I
MILES MAYHEM

That rich smell of bacon and eggs smothered with the finest of cheddar cheeses meant some bad news was coming my way.

Wait.

The cheddar nipped my eyes as much as it nipped the tongue. No. Burned as much as the thought of losing to pa's blade master skills once more, later today.

No. Wait. I knew this burn, and knew it well.

It burned my tongue and eyes as wonderfully as the sight of the town beauty, that blonde peaches and cream delight for the eyes and loins, Vivian Forester did in that public bath yesterday. Best slim busty beauty ever. Even if her long lush golden hair shielded most of her from my gaze. That could only mean ...

Spiced *cheddar?!*

As in spiced with double doom boom peppers. The kind of peppers that killed lesser men by smell alone.

The best, most expensive kind of spiced cheddar in the whole entire kingdom of Green Shard, and all the villages around, especially including my own village, Green Haven. For miles and miles around. Maybe even one of the best in all seven kingdoms of the Rainbow of Shards.

So not just bad news.

Very bad news.

Yet my eyes were already tearing in joy and delighted agony, and I had only just gotten up.

But not in bed.

My ass was on the floor and my back to the bedroom door. A solid oak door. One that loved to squeak like it was full of celebrating mice nowadays. Least the hardwood floor was swept clean ... mostly clean. Okay. Plenty of dirt already?

Despite the whole train-my-Martial-Art-of-the-Phantom-Saber by learning to sweep the floor right and perfectly each and every day.

Pa would be so disappointed.

But not as disappointed as I was with myself. I was so sure I swept up last night too. A good while of sweeping before heading to bed.

Enough that the dark cherrywood floor should have shined sparkling clean.

The broom was right beside my bed. Where I left it. Its bristles of hay as straggly as ever. Its long jagged handle of cherrywood was worthy of the wonderfully wicked witch Pa claimed it from a good few decades ago.

A witch that soon afterwards became my mom ...

Only moments from now Pa should start pounding away at the door. He had gotten back from his last demon-hunting journey only yesterday, so double the awful news then, since normally he'd want some nice and quiet R&R.

The kind where I'd be the one cooking instead of him ... that I slept so late, sigh. My fault. Entirely.

But that latest dime dreadful was a real page-turner. Sure, everything that Lord Dreadslayer wrote was, and one reason that over a decade ago that rosy-pink-skinned devil girl Bubbles Grim got me hooked on them over a dare to see who could find the most mistakes in them. The winner serving the loser for a week.

But no. Like usual, that book even got everything about demon-hunting right too.

Least from what I knew of the topic, and that wasn't a small bit either.

Even Jazzy Lazuli got into it.

At the time Jazzy seemed to be a little cute twig of a blonde tomboy. She tagged along everywhere with me, well, over a decade ago, before she got sent training elsewhere far away and hasn't returned yet.

Yet I had no doubt Pa would soon invite me to a grand breakfast so delicious that swallowing the upcoming bad news would be easier than ...

Wait.

The shutters to my window were cracked open? With a view of thick gray fog. Spooky fog that chilled me to the core, despite the muggy morning air. The kind worthy of the rogue demonspawn Pa loved to hunt, kill or capture, and not just for coin.

But my shutters were scratched up. Solid thick scratches. From talons no less. Especially by the latch. That poor, poor latch. It had seen better days.

Far better days.

Not even my crude drawings along the window frame were spared. Not the one of little-kid-me wielding a saber with Pa. Not of the one of Ma watching over us from Heaven on her broomstick.

Only the pentacles along the frame of the window were intact. Unscratched. Just like the pentacle charm I always hung around my neck. All still a crisp charcoaled purple like the day Ma put them there long ago.

Except for all the dirt scattered thick over them.

My hackles shot to the sky—and beyond. Practically saying a hello to mom and back.

A moan came from my bed. A girly moan?

My heart lunged into my throat. Stabbing the roof of my mouth.

Gulp.

Bestill my stupid heart. No chance I got lucky last night. Not when I hadn't scored a dance with any girl at any festival since forever. Too chubby. Too suntanned. Too callused.

Least some of them talked to me. Acknowledged my awkward existence. And more. Plenty more.

Like Vivian Forester, but she was genuinely friendly with everyone, like a good-natured elf girl should be. Not quiet and withdrawn like the erotically gorgeous Fey Skylure. Sure Fey was a harpy with lovely white eagle wings and feathers in cute but unusual places, along with feet like an eagle's, but wow, was she ... shy.

Yes. Shy. Not haughty. As much as it seemed like.

Least according to Vivian. Who was friends with Fey too. Like she was with practically everyone.

Which was how I learned for sure that girls in these parts wanted thin, pale, but firm. Like most nobles were. Proof of wealth and success, supposedly, or at least what girls found cute and handsome.

Nothing like me (yet).

Unlike any noble, I was very much dressed in plain blue slacks, an even bluer vest, but no boots. Not indoors. My soft leather boots were beside the foot of the bed.

Dirt was scattered over them? Not under them.

Someone tossed a bunch of dirt into my room last night. Why and how it didn't wake me ... least I knew I did (probably) swept up and well before the vandal struck.

Phew.

(Kinda.)

So I managed to take a deep breath. But only smelled that rich deceptive breakfast being prepared for me. Pa would be here any moment and that long human-sized lump underneath the covers of the bed ...

I stood up.

Thanks to pa's martial arts training I was dangerous with or without a blade.

So, quietly, I crept over.

The human-sized lump was stirring. Breathing. As if sleeping.

Until I yanked the covers off. A flash of blue.

And no one was there?!

CHAPTER 2
MILES MAYHEM

Knock knock knock. The door. But so what?

My bed. Empty? Really …

My heart raced so fast it could have dashed around all seven kingdoms, the Rainbow of Shards, and not just once. The cock-a-doodle-doo coming from right outside my window—ah, yes, **breath**.

Breathing right was the most important technique I had to master in my training. Calm. Deep. And steady.

Except, no, that freezing cold gust of wind from yanking off the covers, yeah, it hit me an instant later.

And that gust smelled strongly of a peaches and strawberry musk. The kind of gentle but potent musk a town beauty like Vivian or Fey would definitely perfume herself to the beautiful death with before a festival dance—for the right guy. Like Thomas Gray or, even better, Dedrick Knight. Both stallion studs in their own way—according to Vivian and all her friends.

Even if Dedrick was too clueless to notice anything except how to improve our fighting skills together. Never mind the crazy tall Thomas somehow also had so much dwarf blood in him so he only really went for chubby short dwarf girls who, unfortunately, were very rare in these parts.

Wait.

Blink.

Blink blink blink.

The smell vanished as soon as I smelled it. Despite smelling deep and certain.

As certain as I was with a blade.

Even with that rich breakfast smell smothering it away. A breakfast I better not be late for. Pa must have put so much work into it, sigh, I had to have it. Enjoy it. Or else the tears in his eyes wouldn't be just from double doom boom peppers.

Time to face whatever bad news Pa was going to throw at me.

But the indent in my mattress proved someone had slept there too. And not me. Someone ... strangely shaped. Wider. More jagged. It was human-sized but ... maybe not quite human. There were some deep dents in the sheets. Very deep.

As if from spikes. Or dull blades.

But my down pillow had a human-like head indent in it. A few strands of my short black hair too. More than a few here and there. Another cleaning was in order. But wait ...

It couldn't be but ...

A closer look ...

And a couple long golden strands of hair?

No one in this house ever had golden hair. No one. Few people in Green Shard had hair this golden. Only a few town beauties did, actually, like Vivian and Fey, but Fey's was a bit paler yet still utterly gorgeous. No horses either. No animals. No.

Not this golden. Other than Vivian.

I sniffed the pillow, my sheets close up. That gentle yet potent peaches and strawberry musk. Yeah. It was there. And—

Knock knock knock.

Oh no. Pa. What would I say? I was twenty so having a girl in my room wasn't exactly unheard of, well, for me it would be, but for guys my age, not unheard of, not at all, in fact plenty got married by now.

Stepping back—ack! The dirt on my feet. Oh crap. The dirt. There was so much beside my bed. I ... no excuses. I'd just need to sweep up again. No problem.

Just another chance to train even—

"Hey! Miles—"

"Pa! I'll be right out!"

A glance at my nightstand across from bed. At the drawing I made long ago of Ma and Pa and me and—oh. my. *Gods*.

On the waist-high cherrywood nightstand was a girl, and not just any girl, but a girl erotically slim in the best places, and gorgeously obese in the chest places. Sitting with lush legs crossed and kicking gently, as if patiently impatient. In a beautifully brilliant blue dress so snug and skimpy short ...

and **revealing**, really *really* revealing, it was more like undies in public revealing.

Nothing any girl in our village was allowed to wear in public.

Maybe not even in private.

Especially those suggestive pink strings. Keeping those erotic gaps tight while revealing a tight slim tummy and sweet curvy sides and part of that ample, ample bosom that—

Gulp.

Those lips of hers smiled strawberry tart sinister at me. At if saying *finally* without saying a word.

A smirk that reached those huge gorgeous eyes. The left ... a brilliant glowing blue? No, not just blue but a brilliant azure blue. But the other ... a brilliant beaming red? Ruby red. Wow.

And my full-body ogling of her, especially a second longer ogle at those obese jiggling breasts, only got me an annoyed flick of that golden hair. Waist-long hair that still framed her heart of a pixie pretty face so perfectly ... wait.

From her elbows down to her hands ... not brilliant blue leather gloves of the snug and sleek variety that so many girls loved lately, no, it was a part of her. Down to her hands.

Hands that had pink but yet all-too-cute claws?

Same for her knees down to her feet.

And wings!

As wide as her arm span. No. A good bit wider. Brilliant blue dragon wings. Like beautiful bat wings gone exotically serpenty scaled. With pink smudges spread between the ... the ... long finger thingies?

She giggled. Softly.

A demon girl. In my bedroom.

Correction.

An *erotically* **gorgeous** demon girl. In my bedroom. Acknowledging my existence as a guy. A guy with needs and desires. For busty slim beauties.

(Okay. Sort of. A guy could hope.)

((Really, really hope.))

Knock knock knock. My door. Pa.

"Miles? You okay?"

The girl grimaced. Rolled her gorgeously brilliant eyes of blue and red at the door.

She whispered, more like mouthed, "Later. You and me."

Her voice was so bubbly sexy sweet and yet so sinister serious that—ack! A blue blur?

And she was gone!

WANT MORE?

Go to

WANT MORE?

Go to

www.JonathanEvanHudson.com

www.ingramcontent.com/pod-product-compliance
Lightning Source LLC
Chambersburg PA
CBHW030819200726
48288CB00004B/1303